Dear Wayne,

   I hope you l... love reading as much as I loved reading to you. I miss you!

   Love,
   Ms. Thomas
   Christmas 1994

The
SNOWMAN
POSTMAN

by Andy Rector
Illustrated by Donna Lee

Olund Owl, Cassie Cat, and Rob Rabbit love Christmas. "It's Christmas time," said Olund Owl. "Let's put up a wreath."

"Hurry, hurry," said Cassie Cat. "It's cold outside."

"Let's make pudding," said Rob Rabbit. "Chocolate pudding!"

"Let's eat the pudding in front of a fire," said Cassie Cat. "A fire in the fireplace will keep us nice and warm."

"Let's decorate the tree in my front yard," said Olund Owl. "I have lots of ornaments and a big yellow star."

"I have an idea," said Cassie Cat. "Let's build a snowman. We can make him a happy snowman."

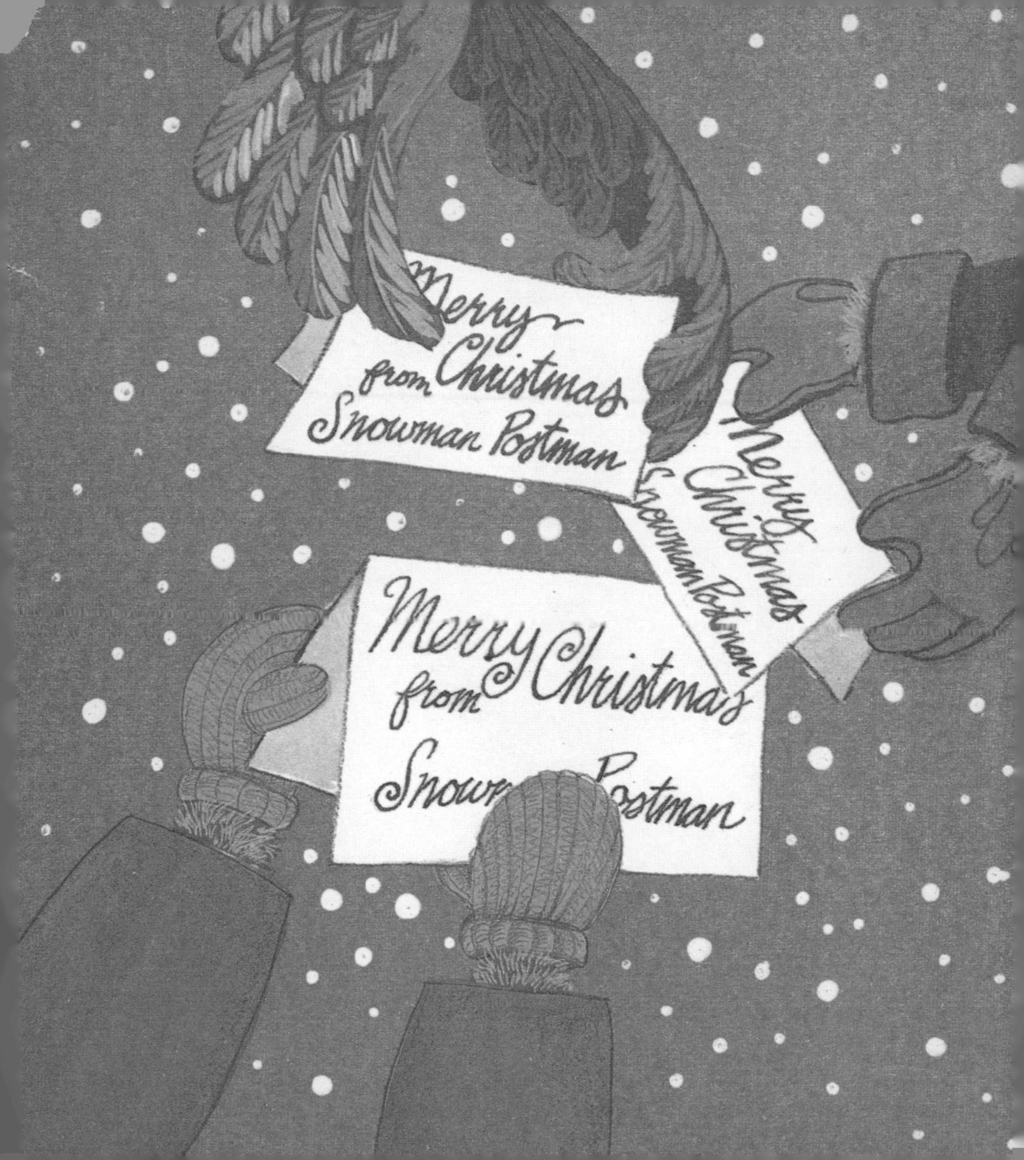

"Well, it's been a fun day," said Olund Owl. "But I'm tired. Let's play together tomorrow. Good night."

   "I will dress our snowman in my grandpa's old postman uniform," said Rob Rabbit. "We can call him our 'snowman postman'!"

"The snowman came to life!" said Cassie Cat.

"Let's ask our new neighbor if he got a card, too," said Rob Rabbit.

"Surprise!" said Farley
Fox. "The cards are really
from me. I want to be your
friend. Won't you come in
for a Christmas treat?"

"My card is from 'The Snowman Postman.'" said Cassie Cat.

"Mine, too," said Olund Owl.

"Mine, too," said Rob Rabbit.

The next day Cassie Cat
ran to meet Olund Owl and
Rob Rabbit. "Look what I
found in my mailbox," said
Cassie Cat. "A Christmas
card."

"Merry Christmas, Farley Fox!" said Olund Owl.
　And they all ate his wonderful chocolate pudding with snowman cookies.